ISBN 1 85854 539 0
First published in Great Britain in 1996 by Brimax
an imprint of Octopus Publishing Group Ltd
2-4 Heron Quays, London, E14 4JP
© Octopus Publishing Group Ltd
Printed in Spain

NURSERY RHYMES

ILLUSTRATED BY
ERIC KINCAID

Brimax

Contents

HUMPTY DUMPTY

Humpty Dumpty sat on a wall,
Humpty Dumpty had a great fall.
All the king's horses and all the king's men,
Couldn't put Humpty together again.

Old King Cole
Was a merry old soul,
And a merry old soul was he;
He called for his pipe,
And he called for his bowl,
And he called for his fiddlers three.

11

THERE WAS A CROOKED MAN

There was a crooked man, and he walked a crooked mile,
He found a crooked sixpence against a crooked stile;
He bought a crooked cat, which caught a crooked mouse,
And they all lived together in a little crooked house.

WEE WILLIE WINKIE

Wee Willie Winkie runs through the town,
Upstairs and downstairs in his nightgown.
Rapping at the window, crying through the lock,
Are the children all in bed, for now it's eight o'clock?

A CAT CAME FIDDLING

A cat came fiddling out of a barn,
With a pair of bag-pipes under her arm;
She could sing nothing but, fiddle cum fee,
The mouse has married the humble-bee.
Pipe, cat; dance, mouse;
We'll have a wedding at our good house.

LITTLE MISS MUFFET

Little Miss Muffet
Sat on a tuffet,
Eating her curds and whey;
There came a big spider,
Who sat down beside her
And frightened Miss Muffet away.

WHAT ARE LITTLE BOYS MADE OF?

What are little boys made of?
What are little boys made of?
Frogs and snails
And puppy-dogs' tails,
That's what little boys are made of.

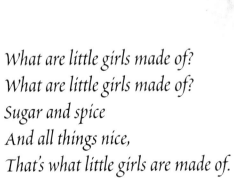

What are little girls made of?
What are little girls made of?
Sugar and spice
And all things nice,
That's what little girls are made of.

HICKETY, PICKETY, MY BLACK HEN

Hickety, pickety, my black hen,
She lays eggs for gentlemen;
Gentlemen come every day
To see what my black hen doth lay.
Sometimes nine and sometimes ten,
Hickety, pickety, my black hen.

DOCTOR FOSTER WENT TO GLOUCESTER

Doctor Foster went to Gloucester
In a shower of rain;
He stepped in a puddle,
Right up to his middle,
And never went there again.

THREE BLIND MICE

Three blind mice, see how they run!
They all ran after the farmer's wife,
Who cut off their tails with a carving knife,
Did you ever see such a thing in your life,
As three blind mice?

THERE WAS AN OLD WOMAN

There was an old woman
Lived under a hill,
And if she's not gone
She lives there still.

THE NORTH WIND DOTH BLOW

The North wind doth blow,
And we shall have snow,
And what will poor robin do then?
Poor thing.
He'll sit in a barn,
And keep himself warm,
And hide his head under his wing.
Poor thing.

MARY HAD A LITTLE LAMB

Mary had a little lamb,
Its fleece was white as snow;
And everywhere that Mary went
The lamb was sure to go.

It followed her to school one day,
That was against the rule;
It made the children laugh and play
To see a lamb at school.

And so the teacher turned it out,
But still it lingered near,
And waited patiently about
Till Mary did appear.

Why does the lamb love Mary so?
The eager children cry;
Why, Mary loves the lamb, you know,
The teacher did reply.

THERE WAS A LITTLE GIRL

There was a little girl, and she had a little curl
Right in the middle of her forehead;
And when she was good, she was very, very good,
And when she was bad, she was horrid.

PETER PIPER

Peter Piper picked a peck of pickled pepper;
A peck of pickled pepper Peter Piper picked;
If Peter Piper picked a peck of pickled pepper,
Where's the peck of pickled pepper Peter Piper picked?

HUSH≈A≈BYE, BABY

Hush-a-bye, baby, on the tree top,
When the wind blows the cradle will rock;
When the bough breaks the cradle will fall,
Down will come baby, cradle, and all.

THERE WAS AN OLD WOMAN

There was an old woman tossed up in a basket,
Seventeen times as high as the moon;
Where she was going I couldn't but ask it,
For in her hand she carried a broom.
Old woman, old woman, old woman, quoth I,
Where are you going to up so high?
To brush the cobwebs off the sky!
May I go with you?
Aye, by-and-by.

LITTLE JACK HORNER

Little Jack Horner
Sat in the corner,
Eating a Christmas pie;
He put in his thumb,
And pulled out a plum,
And said, 'What a good boy am I!'

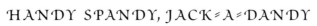

HANDY SPANDY, JACK-A-DANDY

Handy Spandy, Jack-a-Dandy,
Loves plum cake and sugar candy;
He bought some at a grocer's shop,
And out he came, hop, hop, hop.

A WISE OLD OWL

A wise old owl lived in an oak;
The more he saw the less he spoke;
The less he spoke the more he heard.
Why can't we all be like that wise old bird?

I SAW THREE SHIPS

I saw three ships come sailing by,
Come sailing by, come sailing by,
I saw three ships come sailing by,
On New Year's day in the morning.

And what do you think was in them then,
Was in them then, was in them then?
And what do you think was in them then,
On New Year's day in the morning?

Three pretty girls were in them then,
Were in them then, were in them then,
Three pretty girls were in them then,
On New Year's day in the morning.

One could whistle, and one could sing,
And one could play on the violin;
Such joy there was at my wedding,
On New Year's day in the morning.

RIDE A COCK-HORSE TO BANBURY CROSS

Ride a cock-horse to Banbury Cross,
To see a fine lady upon a white horse;
Rings on her fingers and bells on her toes,
And she shall have music wherever she goes.

IF ALL THE WORLD WERE PAPER

If all the world were paper,
And all the sea were ink,
If all the trees were bread and cheese,
What should we have to drink?

THERE WAS AN OLD WOMAN

There was an old woman who lived in a shoe,
She had so many children she didn't know what to do;
She gave them some broth without any bread;
She whipped them all soundly and put them to bed.

I SEE THE MOON

I see the moon,
And the moon sees me;
God bless the moon,
And God bless me.

THE QUEEN OF HEARTS

The Queen of Hearts
She made some tarts,
All on a summer's day;
The Knave of Hearts
He stole the tarts,
And took them clean away.

The King of Hearts
Called for the tarts,
And beat the Knave full sore;
The Knave of Hearts
Brought back the tarts,
And vowed he'd steal no more.

I HAD A LITTLE HEN

I had a little hen,
The prettiest ever seen;
She washed up the dishes,
And kept the house clean.
She went to the mill
To fetch me some flour,
And always got home
In less than an hour.
She baked me my bread,
She brewed me my ale,
She sat by the fire
And told a fine tale.

DIDDLE, DIDDLE, DUMPLING, MY SON JOHN

Diddle, diddle, dumpling, my son John,
Went to bed with his trousers on;
One shoe off, and one shoe on,
Diddle, diddle, dumpling, my son John.

JACK SPRAT

Jack Sprat could eat no fat,
His wife could eat no lean,
And so between them both, you see,
They licked the platter clean.

POLLY PUT THE KETTLE ON

Polly put the kettle on,
Polly put the kettle on,
Polly put the kettle on,
We'll all have tea.

Sukey take it off again,
Sukey take it off again,
Sukey take it off again,
They've all gone away.

Oh, the brave old Duke of York,
He had ten thousand men;
He marched them up to the top of the hill,
And he marched them down again.
And when they were up, they were up,
And when they were down, they were down,
And when they were only half-way up,
They were neither up nor down.

PUNCH AND JUDY

Punch and Judy
Fought for pie;
Punch gave Judy
A knock in the eye.
Says Punch to Judy,
'Will you have any more?'
Says Judy to Punch,
'My eye is sore.'

PEASE PORRIDGE HOT

Pease porridge hot,
Pease porridge cold,
Pease porridge in the pot
Nine days old.

Some like it hot,
Some like it cold,
Some like it in the pot
Nine days old.

ONE, TWO, THREE, FOUR

One, two, three, four,
Mary at the cottage door,
Five, six, seven, eight,
Eating cherries off a plate.

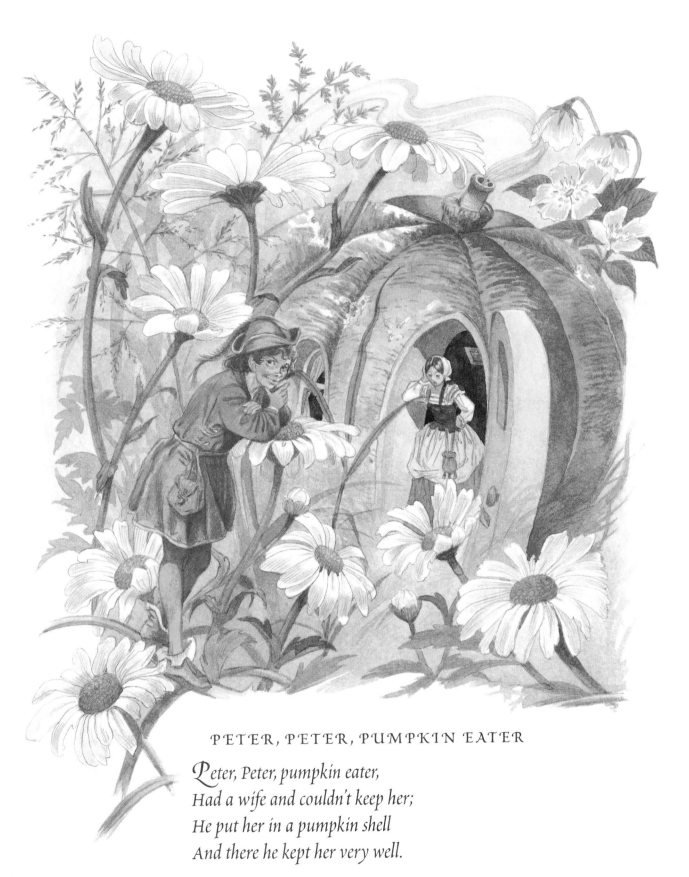

PETER, PETER, PUMPKIN EATER

Peter, Peter, pumpkin eater,
Had a wife and couldn't keep her;
He put her in a pumpkin shell
And there he kept her very well.

Baa, baa, black sheep,
Have you any wool?
Yes, sir, yes, sir,
Three bags full;
One for the master,
And one for the dame,
And one for the little boy
Who lives down the lane.

GOOSEY, GOOSEY GANDER

Goosey, goosey gander,
Whither shall I wander?
Upstairs and downstairs
And in my lady's chamber.
There I met an old man
Who would not say his prayers.
I took him by the left leg
And threw him down the stairs.

THERE WAS A LITTLE BOY

There was a little boy went into a barn,
And lay down on some hay;
An owl came out and flew about,
And the little boy ran away.

Simple Simon met a pieman,
Going to the fair;
Says Simple Simon to the pieman,
'Let me taste your ware.'

Says the pieman to Simple Simon,
'Show me first your penny.'
Says Simple Simon to the pieman,
'Indeed I have not any.'

Simple Simon went a-fishing,
For to catch a whale;
All the water he had got
Was in his mother's pail.

Simple Simon went to look
If plums grew on a thistle;
He pricked his fingers very much,
Which made poor Simon whistle.

He went for water in a sieve
But soon it all fell through;
And now poor Simple Simon
Bids you all adieu.

MARY, MARY, QUITE CONTRARY

Mary, Mary, quite contrary,
How does your garden grow?
With silver bells and cockle shells,
And pretty maids all in a row.

If all the seas were one sea,
What a great sea that would be!
If all the trees were one tree,
What a great tree that would be!
If all the axes were one axe,
What a great axe that would be!
And if all the men were one man,
What a great man that would be!
And if the great man took the great axe,
And cut down the great tree,
And let it fall into the great sea,
What a splish-splash that would be!

JACK AND JILL

Jack and Jill went up the hill
To fetch a pail of water;
Jack fell down and broke his crown,
And Jill came tumbling after.

Up Jack got, and home did trot,
As fast as he could caper,
To old Dame Dob, who patched his nob
With vinegar and brown paper.

ROCK~A~BYE BABY

Rock-a-bye baby,
Thy cradle is green,
Father's a nobleman,
Mother's a queen;
And Betty's a lady,
And wears a gold ring;
And Johnny's a drummer,
And drums for the king.

HEY DIDDLE DIDDLE

Hey diddle diddle,
The cat and the fiddle,
The cow jumped over the moon;
The little dog laughed to see such sport,
And the dish ran away with the spoon.

SIX LITTLE MICE

Six little mice sat down to spin;
Pussy passed by and she peeped in.
What are you doing, my little men?
Weaving coats for gentlemen.
Shall I come in and cut off your threads?
No, no, Mistress Pussy, you'd bite off our heads.
Oh no, I'll not; I'll help you to spin.
That may be so, but you don't come in.

RIDE A COCK-HORSE

Ride a cock-horse
To Banbury Cross,
To see what Tommy can buy;
A penny white loaf,
A penny white cake,
And a two-penny apple-pie.

TWINKLE, TWINKLE, LITTLE STAR

Twinkle, twinkle, little star,
How I wonder what you are!
Up above the world so high,
Like a diamond in the sky.

When the blazing sun is gone,
When he nothing shines upon,
Then you show your little light,
Twinkle, twinkle, all the night.

Then the traveller in the dark,
Thanks you for your tiny spark,
He could not see which way to go,
If you did not twinkle so.

In the dark blue sky you keep,
And often through my curtains peep,
For you never shut your eye,
Till the sun is in the sky.

As your bright and tiny spark,
Lights the traveller in the dark,
Though I know not what you are,
Twinkle, twinkle, little star.

OH WHERE, OH WHERE HAS MY LITTLE DOG GONE?

Oh where, oh where has my little dog gone?
Oh where, oh where can he be?
With his ears cut short and his tail cut long,
Oh where, oh where is he?

PUSSY CAT MOLE

Pussy Cat Mole jumped over a coal
And in her best petticoat burnt a great hole.
Poor Pussy's weeping, she'll have no more milk
Until her best petticoat's mended with silk.

SEE-SAW, MARGERY DAW

See-saw, Margery Daw,
Jacky shall have a new master;
Jacky shall have but a penny day,
Because he can't work any faster.

Little Polly Flinders
Sat among the cinders,
Warming her pretty little toes;
Her mother came and caught her,
And whipped her little daughter
For spoiling her nice new clothes.

THE OLD WOMAN

The old woman must stand at the tub, tub, tub,
The dirty clothes to rub, rub, rub;
But when they are clean, and fit to be seen,
She'll dress like a lady, and dance on the green.

ONE, TWO, THREE, FOUR, FIVE

One, two, three, four, five,
Once I caught a fish alive,
Six, seven, eight, nine, ten,
Then I let it go again.

Why did you let it go?
Because it bit my finger so.
Which finger did it bite?
This little finger on the right.

SING A SONG OF SIXPENCE

Sing a song of sixpence,
A pocket full of rye;
Four and twenty blackbirds
Baked in a pie.

When the pie was opened,
The birds began to sing;
Was not that a dainty dish
To set before the king?

The king was in his counting house,
Counting out his money;
The queen was in the parlour,
Eating bread and honey.

The maid was in the garden,
Hanging out the clothes,
There came a little blackbird,
And snapped off her nose.

THIS IS THE HOUSE THAT JACK BUILT

This is the house that Jack built.

This is the malt
That lay in the house that Jack built.

This is the rat,
That ate the malt
That lay in the house that Jack built.

This is the cat,
That killed the rat,
That ate the malt
That lay in the house that Jack built.

This is the dog,
That worried the cat,
That killed the rat,
That ate the malt
That lay in the house that Jack built.

This is the cow with the crumpled horn,
That tossed the dog,
That worried the cat,
That killed the rat,
That ate the malt
That lay in the house that Jack built.

This is the maiden all forlorn,
That milked the cow with the crumpled horn,
That tossed the dog,
That worried the cat,
That killed the rat,
That ate the malt
That lay in the house that Jack built.

This is the man all tattered and torn,
That kissed the maiden all forlorn,
That milked the cow with the crumpled horn,
That tossed the dog,
That worried the cat,
That killed the rat,
That ate the malt
That lay in the house that Jack built.

This is the priest all shaven and shorn,
That married the man all tattered and torn,
That kissed the maiden all forlorn,
That milked the cow with the crumpled horn,
That tossed the dog,
That worried the cat,
That killed the rat,
That ate the malt
That lay in the house that Jack built.

This is the cock that crowed in the morn,
That waked the priest all shaven and shorn,
That married the man all tattered and torn,
That kissed the maiden all forlorn,
That milked the cow with the crumpled horn,
That tossed the dog,
That worried the cat,
That killed the rat,
That ate the malt
That lay in the house that Jack built.

This is the farmer sowing his corn,
That kept the cock that crowed in the morn,
That waked the priest all shaven and shorn,
That married the man all tattered and torn,
That kissed the maiden all forlorn,
That milked the cow with the crumpled horn,
That tossed the dog,
That worried the cat,
That killed the rat,
That ate the malt
That lay in the house that Jack built.

THIS LITTLE PIG WENT TO MARKET

This little pig went to market,
This little pig stayed at home,
This little pig had roast beef,
This little pig had none,
And this little pig cried,
Wee-wee-wee-wee-wee,
All the way home.

ONCE I SAW A LITTLE BIRD

Once I saw a little bird
Come hop, hop, hop,
And I cried, 'Little Bird,
Will you stop, stop, stop?'

I was going to the window
To say, 'How do you do?'
But he shook his little tail
And away he flew.

LITTLE BO-PEEP

Little Bo-Peep has lost her sheep,
And can't tell where to find them;
Leave them alone, and they'll come home,
And bring their tails behind them.

Little Bo-Peep fell fast asleep,
And dreamt she heard them bleating;
And when she awoke, she found it a joke,
For they were still all fleeting.

Then up she took her little crook,
Determined for to find them;
She found them indeed, but it made her heart bleed,
For they'd left their tails behind them.

It happened one day, as Bo-Peep did stray
Into a meadow hard by,
There she espied their tails side by side,
All hung on a tree to dry.

She heaved a sigh, and wiped her eye,
And over the hillocks went rambling,
And tried what she could, as a shepherdess should,
To tack again each to its lambkin.

HOW MANY MILES TO BABYLON?

How many miles to Babylon?
Three score miles and ten.
Can I get there by candle-light?
Yes, and back again.
If your heels are nimble and light,
You may get there by candle-light.

HOT CROSS BUNS!

Hot cross buns!
Hot cross buns!
One a penny, two a penny,
Hot cross buns!
If your daughters do not like them
Give them to your sons;
But if you haven't any of these pretty little elves
You cannot do better than eat them yourselves.

Two little dicky birds
Sitting on a wall;
One named Peter,
The other named Paul.

Fly away, Peter!
Fly away, Paul!

Come back, Peter!
Come back, Paul!

PUSSY CAT, PUSSY CAT

Pussy cat, pussy cat, where have you been?
I've been to London to look at the queen.
Pussy cat, pussy cat, what did you there?
I frightened a little mouse under her chair.

LADYBIRD, LADYBIRD

Ladybird, ladybird,
Fly away home,
Your house is on fire
And your children all gone;
All except one
And that's little Ann
And she has crept under
The warming pan.

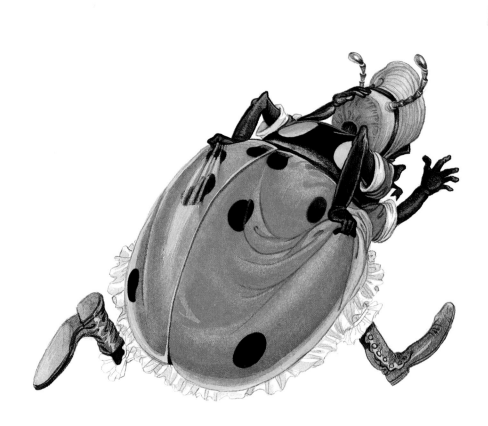

LITTLE BOY BLUE

Little Boy Blue,
Come blow your horn,
The sheep's in the meadow,
The cow's in the corn.
But where is the boy
Who looks after the sheep?
He's under a haystack,
Fast asleep.
Will you wake him?
No, not I,
For if I do,
He's sure to cry.

AS I WAS GOING TO ST. IVES

As I was going to St. Ives,
I met a man with seven wives,
Each wife had seven sacks,
Each sack had seven cats,
Each cat had seven kits,
Kits, cats, sacks and wives,
How many were going to St. Ives?

RING-A-RING O'ROSES

Ring-a-ring o'roses,
A pocket full of posies,
A-tishoo! A-tishoo!
We all fall down.

THREE LITTLE KITTENS

Three little kittens they lost their mittens,
And they began to cry,
Oh, mother dear, we sadly fear
That we have lost our mittens.
What! LOST YOUR MITTENS, YOU NAUGHTY KITTENS!
Then you shall have no pie.
Meow, meow, meow.
No, you shall have no pie.

The three little kittens they found their mittens,
And they began to cry,
Oh, mother dear, see here, see here,
For we have found our mittens.
Put on your mittens, you silly kittens,
And you shall have some pie.
Purr-r, purr-r, purr-r.
Oh, let us have some pie.

The three little kittens put on their mittens,
And soon ate up the pie;
Oh, mother dear, we greatly fear
That we have soiled our mittens.
What! Soiled your mittens, you naughty kittens!
Then they began to sigh,
Meow, meow, meow.
Then they began to sigh.

The three little kittens they washed their mittens,
And hung them out to dry;
Oh! mother dear, do you not hear
That we have washed our mittens?
What! Washed your mittens, then you're good kittens,
But I smell a rat close by.
Meow, meow, meow.
We smell a rat close by.

YANKEE DOODLE CAME TO TOWN

Yankee Doodle came to town,
Riding on a pony;
He stuck a feather in his cap
And called it macaroni.

DING, DONG, BELL

Ding, dong, bell,
Pussy's in the well.
Who put her in?
Little Johnny Green.
Who pulled her out?
Little Tommy Stout.
What a naughty boy was that,
To try to drown poor pussy cat,
Who never did him any harm,
And killed the mice in his father's barn.

COME, LET'S TO BED

Come let's to bed,
Says Sleepy-head;
Tarry a while, says Slow;
Put on the pot,
Says Greedy-gut,
We'll sup before we go.